# A Gift For:

_____

# From:

_____

Published by Hallmark Gift Books,
a division of Hallmark Cards, Inc.,
Kansas City, MO 64141
Visit us on the Web at www.Hallmark.com.

Editor: Megan Langford
Art Director: Kevin Swanson
Designer: Scott Swanson
Production Designer: Bryan Ring

ISBN: 978-1-59530-461-2
BOK1190

Printed and bound in China
NOV11

# SUPER ME!

BY KEION JACKSON

ILLUSTRATED BY RAMON OLIVERA

Hallmark
GIFT BOOKS

Jacob was pretty much always afraid. When he was REALLY scared, he got a gulp in his throat.

Every time Jacob's gulps got
started, Grandma told him to stand
up straight, poke his chest out,
and put on a brave face.

**Jacob didn't have a brave face.**

**He just had a nervous face.**

**And an uh-oh-the-ball-is-coming-to-me face.**

**But no brave face.**

So Jacob decided to do something about it. "Grandma," he said, "I need crayons, construction paper, and twelve juice boxes. It's gonna be a long night."

Jacob got right to work and made his very own superhero mask! "I'll wear it when I'm not feeling so super," he told Grandma. "It'll bring my brave out."

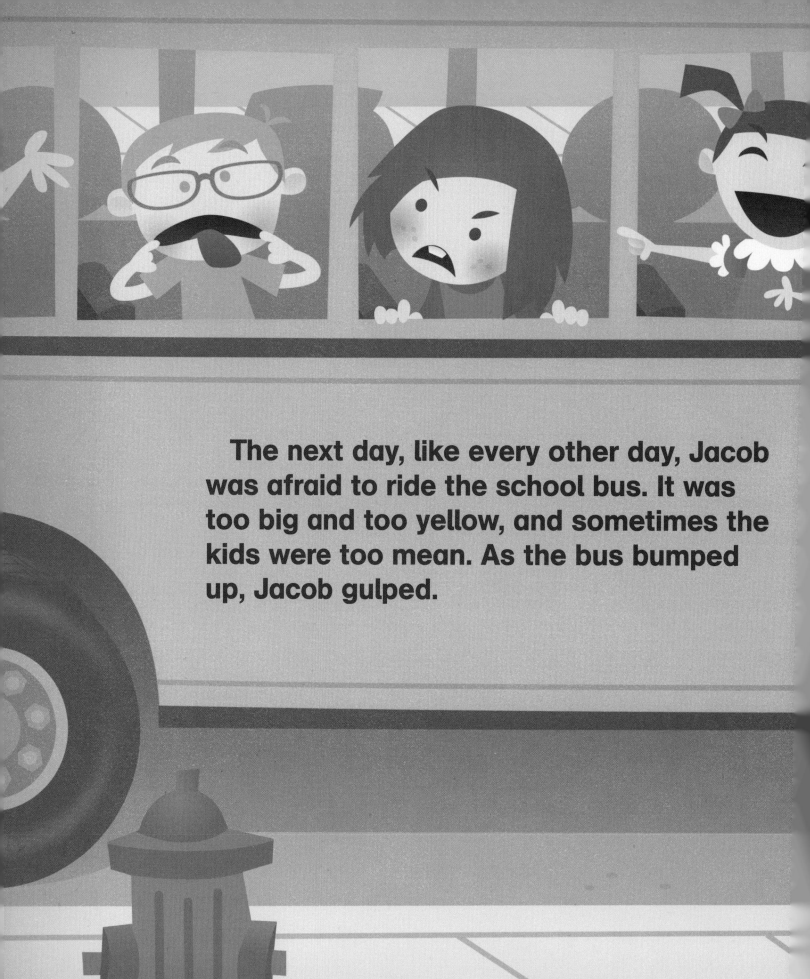

The next day, like every other day, Jacob was afraid to ride the school bus. It was too big and too yellow, and sometimes the kids were too mean. As the bus bumped up, Jacob gulped.

But just as his knees started to knock, Grandma threw him the mask. He put it on and something super happened. Jacob stood up straight and poked his chest out.

Suddenly the bus didn't seem so big or so yellow. He marched right past those sometimes mean kids and bravely took a seat.

At school, Jacob kept his mask close by in case he had to get super. Then, outta nowhere, he heard the scariest two words in the whole wide classroom:

Pop Quiz!

Jacob got a gulp. Spelling was his least favorite subject.

# Paleozoic integrative psychologist baroque onomatopoeia

His brain flooded with words. Big, scary words that he'd only heard people with mustaches use. He didn't know how to spell those words.

Jacob took a deep breath and grabbed his trusty mask. The superness seeped right in. He whipped out a pencil and spelled his way to an A+! A kid named Chester was impressed.

At lunchtime, a mean kid squirted chocolate milk all over Jacob. "A real superhero woulda seen it comin'," he teased. "You ain't so super!" Everybody stared.

Jacob barely noticed.
Superheroes don't mind a
little chocolate milk.

**The lunch lady slapped brussels sprouts on his plate. Jacob was always too afraid to try them. They were balls of yucky nastiness.**

The thought of eating them was scarier than school buses, mean kids, and pop quizzes combined. Jacob got a gulp.

Then he remembered his mask. He could defeat anything with his mask—even brussels sprouts!

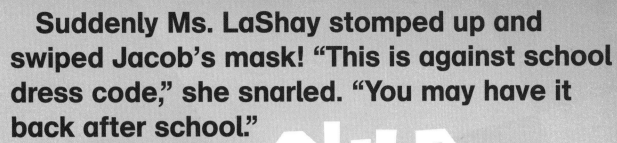

Suddenly Ms. LaShay stomped up and swiped Jacob's mask! "This is against school dress code," she snarled. "You may have it back after school."

Biggest. GULP. Ever.

The super slid right out of him. He could never conquer brussels sprouts without his mask.

Jacob took one look at the sprouts and started gulping. He couldn't stop. They were so green. **GULP.**

And slimy. **GULP.**

And gushy and mushy and moist.

# DOUBLE GULP.

But then he heard Grandma's voice. "Stand up straight!" she said. "Poke your chest out!"

Jacob took one last gulp. He closed his eyes tight, opened his mouth wide, and did the unthinkable.

He tasted.

He chewed.

# HE
# CONQUERED.

**Jacob felt great. He triumphed over brussels sprouts—and he did it WITHOUT the mask!**

After school, Chester looked nervous.
He was learning how to ride a bike,
and the whole thing was making his
belly bubble.

"Take this," Jacob said, handing him the mask. "It'll bring your brave out. Promise to pass it on to another kid once you get braved up."

Jacob knew he would still be afraid of thunder. And eighth-graders. And toilets that flushed by themselves. But he also knew he had some bravery deep down inside—and he could bring it out whenever he needed it the most.

Because Jacob was sometimes afraid. But he was pretty much always super.

**Did you like this book?**
**We would love to hear from you!**

**Please send your comments to:**
**Hallmark Book Feedback**
**P.O. Box 419034**
**Mail Drop 215**
**Kansas City, MO 64141**

**Or e-mail us at:**
**booknotes@hallmark.com**